FriesenPress

Suite 300 - 990 Fort St
Victoria, BC, V8V 3K2
Canada

www.friesenpress.com

ISBN
978-1-5255-4300-5 (Hardcover)
978-1-5255-4301-2 (Paperback)
978-1-5255-4302-9 (eBook)

1. FICTION, AFRICAN AMERICAN, HISTORICAL

Distributed to the trade by The Ingram Book Company

AMADI OHA

"THE GOD OF THUNDER"

PETE J. AMADI, LTCOL

This book is dedicated to people of all faiths, colors, creeds and social status.

Proceeds will go towards building school classrooms for the wonderful children of Terekeka County, Terekeka State, South Sudan.

INTRODUCTION

Are you a proponent of climate change or an advocate of the idea that climate change is a hoax? Do you wonder if there is an alternate truth about why disasters such as hurricanes, tornados, earthquakes and other violence of nature persist in the Western world?

In this book lies the answer to the questions and debate – through the intricate African mythology and deity, Amadi Oha. It is grounded in appeasement to the gods and ancestral veneration, and what happens when an abomination is committed and unending damnation and calamities of enormous proportion are unleashed.

The consequences of not appeasing the gods last for generation after generation. *Amadi Oha! The God of Thunder* eloquently accentuates the abominations and sacrilege meted out against Africans and the African continent in the form of slavery, which desecrated the land and the people, and to which no appeasement has yet been performed by the Western perpetrators.

Many years have gone by with no serious acknowledgment of this evil deed to ancestors or appeasements to the gods; instead, more heinous forms of slavery, including economic enslavement, racial discrimination and other forms of inequality, continue to be meted out against *oha na eze ndi* Africa.

The gods, including Amadi Oha, have remained angry at the West, and from time to time the god of thunder needs to remind the people through hurricanes, tornados, flooding, forest fire and volcanic eruptions such that time is not a healer where sacrilege and abomination are concerned. The desecrated African land must be cleansed and the gods appeased, otherwise the worst is yet to come.

Consideration of appropriate reparation in the form of development, transfer of technology, human dignity and respect could be a start, *Iseeee!!!*

—Adanna Amadi

THE STORMY MESSAGE FROM AMADI OHA

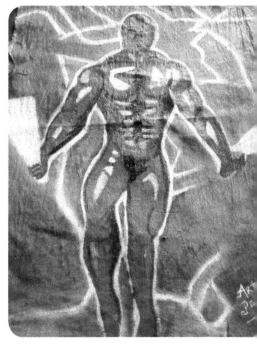

"If these calamities don't stop soon, humanity will suffer the same fate as the dinosaurs," Chinedu said to himself as he watched the cable news show, CNN. "There'll be nothing left of us but skeletal relics." Across the screen flashed bold red letters: BREAKING NEWS! BREAKING NEWS! BREAKING NEWS! HURRICANE IRMA HITS FLORIDA!

Chinedu watched in awe as the reporter detailed the response efforts by the U.S. Federal Emergency Management Authority, known as FEMA, to rescue and evacuate Floridians affected by the hurricane while behind the reporter could be heard a chilling cacophony of noises, screams, cries and shouts of "I love you! Try to stay alive! Help is coming!"

A man who appeared to be in his mid-thirties was filmed carrying a four-year-old child on his shoulders. He seemed to be shaken to his bones as he struggled to wade through the waters. His head was barely above the water; the rest of his body, submerged. With upraised hands, he balanced the child on his shoulders above the ever-rising water. Should he make a wrong move as he struggled on, only God and luck would save them.

"The man might survive, but the child will definitely drown," Chinedu thought in horror.

He agonized about what he was watching, fully aware that nothing good would come out of it, for he had seen things like this before. His mind wandered back to his village several years ago when he was just eight years old.

On that fateful day, Abo village was battling a debilitating torrential rain with heavier-than-usual thunderstorm and lightning; it destroyed peoples' lives. The heavy rain flooded farmlands and houses, creating water logs, wreaking havoc all over the place. The nightmare continued unabated for several hours that, to the villagers, seemed an eternity. The rain came relentlessly for three days. On the morning of the fourth day, the rains seemed to abate and the Abo council of elders, through the town crier, ordered people to stay indoors until libations to appease the gods were completed.

Chinedu remembered his mother muttering repeatedly all through the unceasing deluge, "The gods are angry again!" When he asked his mother why the gods were so angry and so provoked that they would resort to wreaking havoc on and bringing despair to the people they were supposed to protect, his mother had responded, "When you grow older, you will understand."

He had since grown but still found it difficult to understand. As a Christian and a regular churchgoer, he was still mystified about why these tragedies continued to occur within the human community.

"The gods are really angry," he thought, "but why?" Chinedu had always considered himself a deeply religious person but even so he tried to rationalize developments and the realities of life until skepticism had also built up in him.

As he ruminated over these issues, one of the hymns that had always struck him as deeply profound drifted into his consciousness. He muttered the words under his breath, his skepticism becoming ever more pronounced:

"By and by, by and by, when the morning comes, when the saints of God are gathered home, we'll tell the story of how we've overcome, for we'll understand it better by and by."

Chinedu felt disillusioned by the song's notion of "better by and by."

"How does this stand true with all these adversities confronting the human community?" he asked himself. He found it harder by the day to reconcile the realities of everyday tragedies and disturbances in the world with the "better by and by" of the church hymn.

He looked up at the television screen again to watch the news. According to the CNN reporter, "Days after it began its assault on the Caribbean and Southern Florida coastline, Hurricane Irma has continued its destructive engagements as it heads north, causing fresh damage in areas where many displaced Floridians sought refuge over the weekend." She paused briefly to catch her breath and then continued.

"The storm's rainbands reached out hundreds of miles beyond its center, and by Monday morning were wreaking unfathomed havoc throughout much of Georgia and South Carolina. Storm surges have made matters worse and compounded the initial problems created by flash flooding since Irma's effects arrived at high tide." The reporter rounded off her segment before introducing an interview with Florida State Governor Rick Scott.

The governor appeared completely beaten and dejected as he spoke to a group of journalists about how the state of Florida had been thoroughly brutalized by the hurricane. Sixty-two percent of the state's residents remained without power. In addition, Northern Florida, including the city of Jacksonville, was experiencing major flooding. The hurricane had killed at least forty-two people since it began a few days earlier.

Chinedu stayed glued to the TV screen so he wouldn't miss out on the possible cause of the tragic event.

"At times, it can be unnerving to watch CNN," he thought. "Especially when the so-called panel of experts invited by the network inject their uninformed opinions as a true analysis of the causes and effects of the situation at hand." He knew he was being harsh, but it was what he felt. "They ought to be presenting these analyses as objectively as possible," he said emphatically, "and as personal opinions." He lingered in his thoughts for a moment, wondering why the station would bring a group of strangers, mostly male and sometimes a token female, to opinionize and analyze the emotional states of victims and relatives of tragic incidents such as massive floods, fires, earthquakes and airplane crashes. Indeed, he saw the futility of it.

"What relief will it offer the victims?" he asked. Chinedu had come to the conclusion that an ordinary security guard – considered the lowest form of employment in Nigeria – would do a far better job analyzing current events than most of the so-called security analysts and experts CNN invited to the show whenever there were incidents of natural disasters, terrorist attacks or such issues.

Chinedu laughed in derision. He was actually feeling bad unnecessarily since the CNN report was sometimes presented in a variant of English that made it difficult for him to understand everything said. Most times he simply feigned understanding to appease his elite uncle, in whose house he lived; his uncle was an ardent listener and patron of the CNN news channel. So, even when his whole countenance and overall appreciation of the news channel was low, he dared not touch the remote control to change the channel while his uncle was in the house. Even when the man was not in the sitting room, Chinedu was aware that wherever he was in the building, his ears were primed to hear the CNN channel.

The memory of one fateful day rose up. The day he tried to change the channel to watch a series on Africa Magic – a collection of shows dominated by Igbo cultural dramas, which most African households couldn't get enough of – instead of CNN remained ever fresh in his mind.

All his friends watched nothing but the Africa Magic television network in their homes; he so wished it would be the case at his uncle's house as well. That day, thinking he was alone, Chinedu changed the channel to Africa Magic and reclined back on the sofa. But no sooner had he done that than his uncle bellowed from the adjoining room to turn back to the CNN channel. Chinedu was shocked. He did not know that his uncle was listening. Since then, he'd refrained from such acts to avoid being reprimanded.

Chinedu's uncle, Mr. Sam, was a renowned reporter and an editor of *The Reporter* magazine. *The Reporter* was the most popular, and unarguably the most influential, news magazine in the country. Chinedu's entire family was very proud of their illustrious son, Mr. Sam. The entire extended family was in the habit of dropping Mr. Sam's name as their relative to curry favor whenever they were in need or in a problematic situation that required the input of an influential person.

Chinedu was greatly favored among his friends because he shared the same last name as Mr. Sam Agu.

In a country where the *ima mmadu* syndrome had become a regular engagement, influential moves were an asset. *Ima mmadu* was the tendency to drop names of influential people, particularly the rich and politicians; people connected to them were usually treated with respect in the public domain, especially with law enforcement officers and civil servants.

For the well-connected, it was normal to receive preferential treatment even from the most corrupt agency of the government. For law enforcement officers, such as the police, and other paramilitary agencies, such as civil defense and immigration, any person with such connections was given unsolicited attention. Being a nephew to Mr. Sam Agu, the editor-in-chief of *The Reporter*, Chinedu Agu benefited from such recognition. So, for such favors, he was grateful to Mr. Sam, who he simply called Uncle Sam. He revered him and therefore never bothered again to change the TV channel away from CNN. "After all," he reasoned, "as a journalist, the man is keeping himself up to date with the news network."

Chinedu recalled the day he was riding with Uncle Sam when their vehicle was stopped by policemen at a checkpoint. That day offered Chinedu the opportunity to understand the social worth of his uncle. At the check point, once the officers recognized Mr. Sam Agu, rather than indulge in the usual tantrum aimed at extorting money from motorists, the officers instead saluted and shouted, "*Shun, sa!*" with much emphasis on the "sir" pronounced as "saa" to show great respect for his uncle, the influential editor.

As Chinedu returned his attention the unfolding events on CNN, he saw the Florida governor was on the air again being interviewed by CNN reporters.

"It sounds kind of counterintuitive that we'd have that, because the center of the storm is over two hundred miles away in Western Georgia, and here we are below the coast of South Carolina." There was a pause after which the governor continued. "But just if you looked at the bigger weather map and saw the counterclockwise rotation of Irma, juxtaposed with a clockwise high-pressure rotation over the Atlantic, Charleston was in the pincer of those two motions that have driven wind and hurricane bands almost directly into our city." The governor's tone was full of sadness over the unfortunate development.

Earlier in the week, Chinedu heard Mr. Sam talking with one of his visitors about a community in a faraway land that was almost overrun by floodwater. However, he did not quite remember the name of the place but it sounded like "flower," and he wondered which location on earth had that sort of funny name.

During their conversation, Chika, Mr. Sam's friend, spoke of how the floodwater was so vicious it pulled down trees, which fell against a house, killing the entire family who were sleeping in the house. Many buildings were destroyed beyond repair within the same city.

"My friend Mr. James Carlton's home was also destroyed by the storm. His was in the Jacksonville area," Chika said. "If not for the insurance company, I don't know how he would have rebuilt his life again."

Mr. Sam seemed to reflect on the information. Then he cut in, "My sympathy is for a former colleague, Mike Carpenter." Mike had recently retired from the United States Marine Corps after serving honorably for thirty years in order to take care of his fifteen-year-old daughter, Brook, who was suffering from a debilitating disease that had left her completely paralyzed from the waist down. "I was told that he watched in disbelief as chunks of a three-story building where

7

he had a condominium that was destroyed by the storm were swept away by floodwater."

As Sam and his friend chatted away, Pa Ikedi, a frequent and always-welcome visitor who lived in the neighborhood, entered. Pa Ikedi had been a very close friend of Uncle Sam and his family for as long as Chinedu could remember. He knew very well that what Pa Ikedi lacked in material wealth, he made up for with the richness of his words and wisdom. Uncle Sam had enormous respect for Pa Ikedi.

The elderly man was not really too old, as he could still walk briskly whenever the occasion demanded. Chinedu knew that the man maintained a healthy, steady relationship with Uncle Sam. And so, it was not surprising to see Pa Ikedi in Uncle Sam's house. Chinedu was aware that Uncle Sam had developed the habit of consulting Pa Ikedi for advice before making investment decisions. Their relationship was so strong and positive that sometimes Chinedu wondered if Pa Ikedi had this strong hold on Uncle Sam out of mere interest or if there was some magic spell.

Because of this, whenever Pa Ikedi walked into the house, Chinedu knew to let him in immediately. He was the one visitor who should never be kept waiting at the door.

Pa Ikedi always had views that he liked to discuss and the occasion of the current storm was no different. At times, Chinedu found Pa Ikedi's views and experiences ridiculous and unbelievable, but the old man could not be cajoled into jettisoning his opinions.

Pa Ikedi attributed the socioeconomic problems currently afflicting Nigeria and posing problems for the Nigerian masses to the cultural event back in 1977 that became known as FESTAC 77. Chinedu could vividly recall, even though he had been a young boy in his primary school days, the year Nigeria hosted the first-ever Festival of

Arts and Culture that had the internationally acclaimed acronym of FESTAC 77.

Pa Ikedi had always argued that, during the festival, "strange gods" brought by many African countries and other black people from other countries to Lagos were the root cause and genesis of the country's problems. Chinedu doubted Uncle Sam actually believed Pa Ikedi's incredible story. However, whether Uncle Sam believed it or not, it didn't really matter, as he would not argue with Pa Ikedi over any issue; he respected him too much. And Pa Ikedi himself would always press the idea of his age and supposed wisdom with the constant refrain he always uttered while speaking with Uncle Sam:

"What an old man sees while sitting may not even be seen by a child while standing," and Uncle Sam would always laugh to show his positive acceptance.

2 WISDOM OF
THE OLD ONE

Despite Chinedu's thoughts about Pa Ikedi's tales, he remained very fond of the old man and his great sense of humor. That was why Chinedu liked him so much. This fondness did not exist with Chinedu alone. Uncle Sam's children and the other children within the neighborhood equally adored Pa Ikedi. They usually gathered around him at sunset to listen to his exciting stories.

Chinedu recalled one particular day when one of the children, Chimezie, saw Pa Ikedi, who had come to visit Uncle Sam, and called out, "Mazi! Mazi! Please tell us a story."

Pa Ikedi had laughed and retorted, "If I tell you a story at this time of the day, I will die."

The frightened boy looked at him and asked, "Why, mazi?"

Pa Ikedi pointed to the sky and said, "Because you don't tell stories with the sun still up there." Then the old man simply looked away, fully engrossed in other matters as though nothing had happened.

The incident had left a remarkable impression on Chinedu. He reflected on the truth of Pa Ikedi's assertion about the sun and storytelling but did not pursue the matter with him.

However, once the sun had gone to sleep, the children all came out to hear Pa Ikedi's exciting stories.

"I won't tell you stories about the tortoise tonight," Pa Ikedi started as the group of youngsters gathered around.

One of the children, Yemi, who lived three houses away from Uncle Sam's house asked, "Can you finish the story of the chicken and the duck?"

Pa Ikedi responded, "I did finish it when I told the story of why the hawk does not attack the ducklings but, instead, attacks the chicks." The other children nodded in approval; Yemi had not been around for the story that night.

Pa Ikedi then continued. "Today I will tell you children a story about where you all come from but, first, let me ask you all. Where are you from?" Pa Ikedi looked straight into the eyes of the children seated in a semicircle facing him.

"I am from Agbor!" one child shouted.

"I am from Isiala," another said.

The chorus of answers continued for about a minute, but soon there was silence.

"You are all correct," Pa Ikedi said, "but also not correct." He sent the children a superior look to show his confidence in the matter. "You are all correct in the sense that the places you have all mentioned are places you have been told by your parents that you are from. Unfortunately, that is not entirely true.

"If you can think back, you will remember that a long, long time ago, when the shadows stood still and the night refused to yield for daylight, when the owls refused the offer of chicks while bats basked in daylight flights, a great sacrilege was committed against your land." Pa Ikedi stopped to catch his breath.

One of the children asked, "What is the meaning of sacrilege?"

"It's an abomination that was committed against this land a very long time ago." Pa Ikedi saw the child's confusion remained and decided to be much simpler. "A sacrilege is an act that society condemns, especially those acts that customs and traditions forbid."

The way Pa Ike went about telling the story drew Chinedu's attention. He noticed that the structure and pattern of Pa Ikedi's tale was much different from the usual folktales of the tortoise and other animals. As a result, even though the audience was mainly children, he sat down in the corner and listened attentively.

"Long time ago," Pa Ikedi started again in his usual manner, "our people lived peacefully and happily together. We organized our societies around families called the *umunna*. Our people had a wide variety of political arrangements including kingdoms, city-states and other organizations, each with their own language and culture. We were hardworking, virtuous, contented and sincere with one another."

Pa Ikedi paused and briefly scrutinized the face of each child. Then he smiled. "We farmed vast lands, fished in great rivers, hunted in great forests for what we eat and sell. We begged no one for anything." He paused again and gauged the attentiveness of each child. Feeling satisfied, he continued.

"Our people made objects from bronze, brass, copper, wood and ivory." Pa Ikedi smiled again in an undisguised expression of joy. He was glad the children trusted his abilities. "We were highly skilled in ivory carvings, pottery, rope and gum production."

One of the children interrupted him. "You forgot to mention their godless attribute. My teacher told me that our forefathers did not know God."

Pa Ikedi smiled. "It is not true that our fathers and mothers did not know God. On the contrary, we had many gods; we could afford so many of them. Our religions were not based on sacred texts or scriptures that promoted the worship of only one deity. There were as many gods and goddesses as there were human communities. In fact, our religious observances even identified that every individual has his own god, which was regarded as the personal *chi*. This is the god responsible for keeping the individual constantly reminded of that which is right or wrong. As were our beliefs and religious observances." Pa Ikedi paused to take a sip from the bottle of water he had stood by his seat.

The children were elated; their eyes shining. They did not blink, as though blinking would make them lose the strand of the story.

"Our people had deep respect and reverence for the gods and ancestral spirits. Astute spirituality was rooted in elevated consciousness." Pa Ikedi adjusted on his seat. "Our gods were one with us and protected us jealously. And if anyone should offend them, we knew quickly how to appease them," Pa Ikedi said triumphantly. He was keen on taking the children on a journey of self-discovery.

"We believed that our ancestors were constantly present to protect us. That is why, whenever I wake up in the morning, I take a glass of palm wine and kola nut to my *Obi* and offer libations and prayers to them." This surprised some of the children, who felt the action was paganish. "It has been working for me," he said with a cheerful grin.

"We did all this before the Arabs invaded our land, and then the Europeans subjugated our people, sold us into slavery and desecrated our land. Sacrileges were committed on our land." Pa Ikedi concluded on a very sad, ominous note, pausing for a moment. Then he heaved a heavy sigh that made one of the children shed some tears.

Pa Ikedi started again. "Our people lived peacefully before the white man arrived at our shores. We had our own ways before they introduced Christianity to us. Have you wondered why water is now disturbing them in *obodo oyibo*, white man's land?" Chinedu was aware of the flood and hurricane situation in Florida but he was not sure if any of the children knew anything about it.

"What water?" one of the children asked.

"I have been hearing for some time now that floodwater and sandstorm have been destroying people's homes in *obodo oyibo*," Pa Ikedi said.

"Do you mean the hurricane?" one child asked.

"Yes. So they call it. They said it has been destroying their houses, shops, farms and other property owned by people in different towns over there," Pa Ikedi asserted.

"Long time ago," he continued, "our land was defiled. The blood of innocent people was shed on our land. The best of our young people were taken away. They caused our communities to fight against one another. These communities had no reason to fight themselves, but the white man brought enmity between them just because they wanted to take slaves."

"Slaves!" one child shouted in utter astonishment. "Mazi, you mean slaves?"

"Yes. They took our people in big boats to travel long distances without food or water."

Chinedu of course had heard many slave tales and stories, and indeed had just watched a movie based on the slave trade called *Roots*. A character named Kunta Kinte was the protagonist. However, he did not really believe anyone could possess the resilience or dexterity needed to survive such conditions as depicted in the movie. So, he kept quiet and listened to Pa Ikedi exchange questions and answers with the children.

"So, did they die?" a child asked.

"Some died. Some did not."

"O God!" one child exclaimed in amazement and burst into tears, whereupon other children joined in the crying. Pa Ikedi started stretching his knuckles and waited silently for the children to quiet themselves. The older children among the group gently tapped the shoulders and patted the backs of the younger children who were crying. It was so touching, but Chinedu kept his cool and his distance from Pa Ikedi and the children buzzing around him.

When the children were calmer and Pa Ikedi was sure they were more composed, he continued with his story.

"They flogged, they maimed, they raped our women, they caused great pains on our land and killed our people with reckless abandon. Now our gods are angry with them greatly. Remember what I said earlier. Our gods protected us jealously and we appeased them immediately anytime someone wronged them or violated our norms.

"In the past, whatever sacrilege that was committed, no matter how grave the issue, it would have been remedied by appeasing the gods. However, only the sons and daughters of the soil with knowledge of the land, norms and temperament of the gods would recognize the right things to do to avoid the impending danger and calamities that ensue for failure to appease the land, the ancestors and the gods.

"Normally, as soon as we discover that the gods are angry, we know what to do. But neither the Arabs nor the Europeans realize these long-held, time-tested practices and spiritual engagements hold our lands together. Neither before then nor even now has the land been left without being appeased. Therefore, the original sin, the abomination, was never remedied. So the burden and consequences persist without the colonizers realizing or caring to find out the root cause. They have offended the gods. Amadi Oha is angry and things continue to fall apart in the land of the white man and will continue until the day they realize the abominations and atrocities they have committed against our land and render the appropriate appeasement to the gods of our land." Pa Ikedi paused to sip his water again.

By this time, the children were deeply hooked to the story though they seemed perplexed and shaken. Most of the children looked bewildered; some were dripping cold sweat. Chinedu observed them. In their small innocent faces, their dazed eyes showed they had been deeply excited by the story. Their eyes fixated on Pa Ikedi as if asking him to reel out the story and break it down in a contemporary Mickey Mouse–style so they could begin to make sense of it. They gazed longingly at Pa Ikedi, hoping to understand the story more as he progressed in his rapturous tales of the African past.

Chinedu was so engrossed in the activities that he did not initially hear his name being called by Uncle Sam. "I'm coming, *sa*," he said after the third call from his uncle. As he stood up, Chinedu hoped he would not receive another backhand slap as he had the last time Uncle Sam felt insulted that Chinedu was not listening to him. This time there was no slap but a thunderous voice.

"You heard my voice, *ewu*! Can beer!" demanded Uncle Sam as Chinedu came into his presence.

Upon hearing Uncle Sam's voice, Pa Ikedi ended his story abruptly. But before leaving to join his friend in the sitting room, Pa Ikedi promised the children he would conclude his story at the next gathering of the group, which, he surmised, would be the second of the next two working days, it being *Nkwo*.

MOONLIGHT STORIES

All African folktales always start with "once upon a time" and the usual thunderous chorus of "and time comes" from the audience. Pa Ikedi's once upon a time on this night of *Nkwo* did not start from where he'd left off previously with the children. Instead, his moonlight story like the night itself metamorphosed into an incredibly spidery event; one could not accuse Pa Ikedi of not having moral lessons associated with his stories. Just as all African names have meaning and are significant to the society that gave them, Pa Ikedi's stories all had profound moral lessons. But only those who had the patience to listen through to the end could reap the benefit of knowing what the lessons were.

"Our story tonight," Pa Ikedi began, "is about the spider called Lagertha the Dinta, or Lagertha the powerful hunter.

"Long, long ago, there was a spider named Lagertha, but everyone called her Dinta because she was the most powerful, bravest hunter. She lived among the human beings on earth."

"How?" one of the children asked.

"Well, my dear, things have changed now," Pa Ikedi said. "The spider swung on her webs from tree to tree or ran on her tiny spider legs along on the ground." He let his eyes sweep across the faces of the children who made up his small audience of listeners and then he continued with his tale, his voice weaving a magical story.

*　*　*

In that distant time, no one told stories on earth. Why? No one had any to tell, for the sky god, Ebube, kept them all to himself up in his sky kingdom.

These hidden stories were mainly tales of happiness, sadness and, most importantly, the hidden mysteries of the world. Many creatures at the time, including human beings, begged Ebube to share these stories, but the sky god refused. No one knew why.

Then along came Dinta. She couldn't bear it any longer, not knowing these tales. She became so curious that she decided to pay a visit to Ebube. So off she went to see the sky god. When she arrived, Ebube, the sky god, immediately waved her away.

"You are only a spidery old girl," the sky god said in mockery. "How will you ever pay for my stories?"

Dinta knew better than to argue with the sky god.

"I only wish to know the price," she said to the sky god. "For I don't yet know if I could afford the price." A grin spread over Dinta's face.

Ebube gave out an ominous, echoing laugh and said, "Very well then! I will trade you my stories for four fierce animals of my choice.

"First is the python named Ajuala, the mighty snake that only feeds on human beings.

"Second is Mgbaro, the hornet that makes the sweetest honey, buzzes like a drunken dragon and possesses crazy stings that can paralyze even a god.

"Third is Agu, the leopard whose teeth are as sharp as knives.

"And fourth is the adorable fairy called Adaugo, who remains as invisible as the wind." Ebube felt quite assured that these were very difficult conditions if not impossible tasks.

"That is a high price for the stories," Dinta said, smiling mischievously. "But I'm sure they must be such wonderful tales indeed." Then she bowed and returned to earth.

When she got home, she immediately described to Ragnar, her husband, the encounter with Ebube and his four unreasonable demands.

"I am a no match in strength or speed to these creatures. How can I capture Ajuala?" she asked, not really expecting Ragnar to answer her rhetorical question. "If I make a mistake, he will surely swallow me."

"A python's strength lies in its body, not its brain," said Ragnar. "You must outsmart him from the start." Her husband paused for a moment before continuing. "To do this, you will need a palm branch and some long vines."

They strategies together the rest of the plan to, and she went away to collect all that was needed for the plan. Then she took the branch and the vines to the stream near where Ajuala lived.

Dinta started showering praises on the snake, calling out loudly, "Ajuala is a great python! I'm sure he is longer than this branch." She waved the branch in order to attract the great python's attention.

Meanwhile, Ajuala listened from the leafy shadows, and Dinta's words created confusion in his head. So he slithered out onto the path in arrogant elegance.

"What's that you were saying, spider?" the python asked, proudly swinging from side to side, preening as the king of all long reptiles recognized for his strength.

"I was talking about you," Dinta responded. "You see this branch? My husband and I had an argument; he said that this branch I'm holding is longer than you are. I told him he was wrong. This branch could not be longer than the greatest and strongest snake in the world. But my husband is very stubborn. He never agrees that he's wrong. He said I should come see you and confirm once and for all who is right between him and me."

"Put the branch next to me," said Ajuala. "I will stretch out to my full length. Then we will see who is telling the truth."

Dinta put down the palm branch, and Ajuala leaned against it.

"Well?" Ajuala asked.

"Patience," said Dinta. "I must measure carefully." As she spoke to him soothingly, Dinta carefully bound the python to the branch with the long vines. Over and over, she wound them around him.

"So what have you learned?" Ajuala asked at last.

"Good news!" said Dinta. "I was right. You are a little longer."

Ajuala was as pleased as the greatest snake in the world could be.

"So now you can release me," he said.

"I wish I could," said Dinta. "But there is also bad news. I must take you to Ebube, the sky god. He has a special mission for you."

So Dinta spun a web around Ajuala and carried him off to the sky god.

If Ebube was surprised to see Ajuala, he hid it well.

"I will take the python,'" he said to Dinta, "but you are not done yet."

"Yes, I know," Dinta said. "But life is one step at a time."

Dinta returned home to share the news with her Ragnar.

"All is well," she said.

"And yet your face is long," her husband replied.

"What can I do about Mgbaro?" Dinta asked Ragnar. "I cannot wrap them in vines."

Her husband nodded. "Hornets that buzz and sting will slip through even nimble fingers. But hornets are nervous and quick to worry," he said in an assured voice. "First, you must fill an empty gourd with water."

Dinta agreed. After she filled the gourd, she went walking through the forest.

Bzzzzzzzzzzzzz.

Dinta heard Mgbaro buzzing overhead. She climbed up a tree above them and sprinkled some water from the gourd onto their nest.

The hornets buzzed louder.

"The rain is coming! The rain is coming! We will all get terribly wet!" the hornets buzzed excitedly.

Dinta cut a large leaf from the tree and held it over her head. Then she took the rest of the water and poured it over the leaf.

"The rain is falling!" Dinta shouted, as the water dripped all around her and made her seem drenched.

"But what can we do?" the hornets asked in confusion.

"You are lucky I am here," said Dinta. "If you come inside my gourd, the rain will not reach you."

The hornets did not hesitate. They flew right into the gourd. When they were all inside, Dinta plugged up the gourd and spun a web around it.

"You will be very safe from the rain now," she said. Then she returned again to Ebube, the sky god, in his kingdom.

The sky god took Mgbaro as he had taken Ajuala.

"I will take the hornets," he said to Dinta, "but you are not done yet."

Again Dinta nodded and returned home.

"What can I do about Agu?" she asked Ragnar, her loyal and loving husband, once again. "I cannot wrap him in vines or catch him in a gourd. And his teeth are as sharp as knives," she said in a tone of exasperation tinged with hope that if they both brain storm together, they will surely have a way out of the task as they had on the earlier ones.

"It would be wise to keep him at a safe distance," said her husband. "You must start with a large hole."

Dinta nodded. She knew exactly what her husband meant, as she had dug such holes before.

Dinta returned to the jungle and found Agu's tracks. There, she dug a deep hole and then covered up the hole with leaves, so it was hard to see.

The next morning, Dinta returned to the hole. Agu was prowling around at the bottom.

"What has happened here?" Dinta asked.

Agu growled at her, showing teeth like knives.

"What do you think? I did not see this hole in the darkness, and I fell in."

"How unlucky," said Dinta. "This should be a lesson to you not to wander around in the dark."

"I do not care about lessons now," said Agu. "I care about getting out. Whoever dug this hole will return soon to take me away, so I need to get out of here as fast as I can."

"Perhaps I can help," said Dinta. "I see some long sticks here. If I lower them down, maybe you can climb up on them."

"Hurry!" said Agu. "We may not have much time."

So Dinta put down the sticks, and Agu placed his paws on them.

"The sticks are wobbly," he complained.

"I am doing the best I can," said Dinta. "You must stay low, keeping your head down and holding on tight."

Agu crept up the sticks, keeping his head down.

When he was very near the top of the hole and almost out, Dinta hit him on the head with a club. Agu groaned and fainted. Quickly, Dinta spun her strongest web around the leopard and the sticks.

"What are you doing?" Agu asked in perplexity when he awoke. "There is no escape! Whoever dug this hole must be very near by now. Don't you understand?"

"True enough," Dinta admitted, "for I must take you to Ebube, the sky god. He has a special mission for you. Isn't that better than being stranded in a ditch with no one in sight?" Dinta asked as she carried him off securely tied to the sticks.

When Dinta returned to the sky god, Ebube was not surprised to see her for he had grown used to the fact that Dinta was capable of anything.

"I will take the leopard," he said, "but you are not done yet."

Dinta was happy she had captured three of Ebube's creatures and was gradually qualifying herself for the star prize of being let into Ebube's pot of wisdom. But how would she ever capture Adaugo?

"How do I find Adaugo, the invisible fairy?" she asked her husband as she arrived home from Ebube's abode in the midst of the clouds.

"You cannot find her," he said. "You must make her find you."

So Dinta started by carving a wooden doll. When she was done, the doll looked almost real. Dinta covered it with sticky gum from a plant.

Then she took the doll to an Iroko tree, where she knew, according to local legends, the fairies played.

There, she mashed some tasty yams until they became pasty and put them in a bowl, which she placed on the doll's lap. Then she rubbed a second coat of gum all over the doll again, tied a vine to the doll's neck and went off to hide in the bushes.

Before long, Adaugo came by. She saw the doll sitting alone under the Iroko tree and noticed the mashed yams.

"May I have some of your food?" Adaugo asked hungrily.

Dinta immediately pulled on the vine she had tied to the doll's neck, which made the head move in up and down, as if nodding its approval.

Adaugo then proceeded to eat some of the tasty yam. She ate and she ate, and soon the bowl was empty. Adaugo wiped her mouth and stood up.

"Thank you," she said to the doll.

The doll said nothing.

"I said thank you," Adaugo repeated.

The doll remained silent.

"Where are your manners?" Adaugo yelled at the doll. "I have thanked you twice. And you will not answer. This is no way to behave. You need to be taught a lesson." Adaugo was very angry that the person she was so profusely showing gratitude to was treating her with disdain.

Adaugo grabbed the doll's left shoulder in an attempt to pull her up and teach her some lesson. When she tried to pull her hand away, it was held tight on the doll's left shoulder. So she grabbed the doll's right shoulder with her other hand. That too got stuck.

Now Adaugo was really mad. She kicked the doll with one foot and then the other, causing both feet to get stuck as well.

She was a sorry picture of helplessness and looked more like a statue. That's when Dinta stepped out from the bushes.

"What have we here?" she asked.

Adaugo attempted to vanish at once as a fairy would normally do, but that did no good. She had messed up her powers by displaying the base human instinct of anger. She had caught herself in the web of human frailties. She was helpless.

So Dinta spun a web around Adaugo and brought her up to Ebube.

When the sky god saw them, he called together everyone in the kingdom.

"Hear me," he told them. "Dinta has met my price. My stories are now hers to do with as she pleases."

When Dinta got home, she shared the stories with Ragnar, her husband. They laughed and cried and shouted in surprise at the endings of some of the stories.

* * *

"However," said Pa Ikedi, "they did not keep the stories to themselves. They told them to others and still do to this day." He finished in a triumphant display of his mastery of the art of storytelling.

"Did you enjoy the story?" Pa Ikedi asked the children.

"Yes sir, Mazi ndeewoo!" the children shouted in excitement.

THE LIFE OF A SLAVE

Uncle Sam had indeed read about slaves and had seen many slave movies including the famous *Roots* that was based on Alex Haley's book in which the main character Kunta Kinte, a Gambian slave in the Southern United States suffered inhumane torture and abuse from his captors and slave master.

Uncle Sam was appalled beyond words at the sexual atrocities he learned were committed by slave traders during the slavery era – though he knew there still remained many forms of slavery in contemporary times. Uncle Sam oftentimes still related the slavery ordeals and the crafty evil engagements of the slave traders to certain African folktales he'd heard many times from Pa Ikedi, his good friend.

One in particular, Mr. Tortoise's story of rags to riches, always came to his mind whenever he thought about how the Arabs and Europeans outsmarted and inhumanely exploited Sub-Saharan Africans during the slave trading era.

According to Pa Ikedi, a long, long time ago there lived a great king in a land far away. In this land, people and animals lived in perfect harmony and understood one another very well. However, as time went by, things took a very bad turn for the people of the kingdom. Their resources started dwindling, their farmlands became less fertile and they were not able to grow sufficient crops to sustain their people. To make matters worse, their wise king, who through his ingenuity had made the kingdom prosperous over the years, had become feeble with old age.

Uncle Sam shrugged his shoulders in amazement. The story was eerily similar to the events that led to the discovery of the Americas by Christopher Columbus, who was funded by the Spanish Queen Isabella at the time. Although the Native Americans who lived there centuries before the arrival of Columbus never considered themselves lost or needing to be found.

The Europeans were the ones in very bad shape, and they lacked adequate resources to sustain their population. The hardship was compounded by the barbaric and wanton warfare that persisted as kingdom rose against kingdom. As well, the era saw the rise of religious purity and the persecution of so-called witches and pagans. Europe was indeed in a socio-economic debilitated state and everyone was grappling with the terrible situation confronting them – hence the quest for salvation outside the European continent. Christopher Columbus dared to try and the Queen had the resources needed for the quest.

Reflecting on these developments, Uncle Sam saw why the story of the founding of the United States of America by Europeans was really a gripping story of resilience and tenacity of purpose.

Meanwhile, in Pa Ikedi's tale, the king still had a last speck of genius to display before he would give up the ghost. In his infinite wisdom, he thought that a better way to maintain the kingdom and survive the impending calamity they were bound to face if conditions remained unchanged was to find another wise man to marry the princess, his only daughter, and thus succeed the wise king who was soon to die. The king came up with a seemingly impossible scheme. He challenged all within the kingdom that whosoever would accomplish his purpose, presented as a task, would marry the princess and assume the throne as his successor.

The challenge was simply that any person who was able to obtain a wife with a grain of corn as the bride price would be the winner.

Of course everyone in the kingdom thought that it was unreasonable and a mission impossible; therefore, no one bothered to try except for Mr. Tortoise.

* * *

After much preparation, Mr. Tortoise, also known as Mr. T, received a piece of corn from the king and set off on his journey. He passed many lands and rivers, traveling day and night. Several weeks into his travels, he was exhausted and feeling dejected but he remained hopeful knowing that failure was not an option. His motivation was simply the riches that he would inherit when he married the princess and became the king of his land.

Eventually, fate smiled upon him. He came to a town where everyone cultivated corn and raised chickens. He arrived late in the evening, tired and exhausted. He went to the next barn he saw and asked the farmer if he could spend the night there with them.

"Of course," said the kind farmer, "we are open to welcoming people; we love strangers. Make yourself at home. You can eat with us and be on your way in the morning." Mr. T was pleased and accepted the kind offer.

After Mr. T had settled in, he pleaded with the farmer to allow him to store his grain of corn in the same barn where the farmer kept his chickens. Mr. T argued that he did not want his corn to get mixed up with the farmer's corn should he store it in the kind farmer's corn storage barn. The unsuspecting farmer consented to the request.

Of course, Mr. T wanted to store the corn with the chickens knowing full well that his corn would be consumed by the corn-loving chickens. The kind farmer had no reason to be afraid; after all, even if Mr. T's grain was lost, he could very easily replace it.

Very shortly, the night passed and it was daylight again, and Mr. T's piece of corn was gone.

Upon waking up and realizing what had happened (his plan had worked!), Mr. T feigned outrage. He started yelling, crying and attracting the attention of the entire town. He told the people gathered how important the corn was to him. He claimed it was the last gift given to him by his grandmother before she passed on. He swore that he would die without his corn. The kind farmer pleaded with Mr. T and asked him what could be done to compensate him for the lost corn.

Mr. T quietly thought for a moment and then said, "I want nothing but the chicken that ate my corn."

He was taken to the barn and there he selected the biggest of all the chickens in the barn and thereafter continued on his journey with the chicken.

After traveling with the chicken for a few days, Mr. T eventually found a kind goat herder. He pleaded with the old herder for room and board and then convinced him to allow his chicken to rest with the goats for the night because storing the chicken among the goat herder's chickens in their roost would lead to a mix-up. Eventually, just before day break, the chicken was trampled by the goats. This did not surprise Mr. T.

Before the first light of dawn, Mr. T rushed to the goat house, flinging himself on the ground and swearing that his life depended on that chicken.

"This chicken was given to me by my grandmother as a last gift before she died," he sobbed.

The entire villagers gathered and pleaded with Mr. T, asking him what he needed as compensation.

"I want the goat that trampled my chicken" he said.

Mr. T was taken to the goat house, where he selected the best goat among the lot from the kind farmer's herd, and then he continued on his way.

After traveling for many days, Mr. T stumbled upon a ranch with a lot of fat cows. He could not imagine his good fortune. While walking towards the ranch, he whispered to himself how Nneorji, the female god of gifts, had shown him favor in his quest.

"You are the dearest and most beautiful lady that my humble eyes have ever seen in my entire life," Mr. T said to the lady who owned the ranch.

"The frog does not run during the day without being pursued. What brought you to my land and how may I help you, Mr. Tortoise?" asked the lady.

Once again Mr. T went into a long story of how he was exhausted from a long journey and needed a place to pass the night. As usual, he convinced the unsuspecting patroness to allow him to store his goat among the cows, knowing fully well what the result would be in the morning.

Mr. T was the first to wake up at daybreak and the one to notice first what had become of his goat. The goat lay dead, trampled by the happy cows just as Mr. T had expected. Mr. T was rewarded with the biggest and fattest cow from the ranch, and he continued on his journey with his fat cow in tow.

Before long, as he continued traveling across towns and villages, Mr. T stumbled upon a grieving family. The family had just lost their beautiful daughter and were in the process of making arrangements for her burial. Mr. T was able to convince the family to allow him to mourn their child with them. After spending a few days with the family, he applied his trickery on the family. He made them believe that he cared so much about the dead girl (who he did not know when she was alive) that she was too precious and beautiful to be buried in a normal burial ground. He argued that she deserved to be buried near the shrine of the goddess of Ola. However, he was the only one who knew where this shrine was located. He then asked them to keep his beautiful fat cow as a show of good faith while he alone would take the body of the dead girl for burial at the designated shrine. The family consented and off went Mr. T with the dead girl.

After traveling for many days, Mr. T came upon a town full of beautiful maidens. He hid under a tree for hours in order to perfect his plans against the unsuspecting but kind and beautiful people. He dressed up the corpse nicely to the point that it looked very much alive. He waited till the sun went down, and as soon as it was dark enough, he carried the corpse with him to a house he had spotted earlier where several beautiful young maidens lived.

Upon arrival, he pleaded with the family to allow him and his wife to spend the night. He claimed they had traveled all day and were so fatigued that his poor wife has passed out due to exhaustion. He convinced the family to allow his young, exhausted, beautiful wife to sleep with the maidens so she could rest well for she would surely feel better in the morning and they could proceed on their journey.

"Sleeping among other young ladies and maidens will surely rejuvenate my wife," he said, and the unsuspecting family consented to his request.

Lightning struck at the same spot again. Mr. T woke up early as usual knowing his plan as he had crafted it. This time, however, he knew he should not be the first to notice the death, so he waited. After everybody was up and ready for breakfast, he wondered aloud what was holding up his wife. He suggested that one of the maidens should go wake her up.

Lo and behold, the maiden came back with the bad news that his wife was dead.

"Wow, wow ... say that again," demanded Mr. T. "How can my wife be dead? You must be joking!"

He rushed to the room where his wife lay lifeless on the bed. Mr. T flung himself on the ground and yelled at the top of his voice and as hard as he could.

Eventually, the entire community gathered. Everyone got involved and in the end he was asked what he wanted as compensation. Mr. T claimed that in his own homeland, tradition demanded that he should be given another wife, but not just any other wife – she must be the same beautiful maiden who had slept in the bed with his wife. After much deliberation among the kind and generous people of the town, it was agreed that Mr. T should marry the beautiful maiden who had shared the bed with his wife.

Mr. T was very happy with the arrangement; though, the beautiful brave maiden wasn't but was compelled to by her people. Nonetheless, she made herself a promise to eventually return back to her community when the time is right and fight injustice. Mr. T subsequently married the beautiful maiden and left with her to his motherland.

Upon his return, Mr. T was celebrated. The king rewarded him as was promised and in his honor dedicated a special day as a holiday. As a result of Mr. T's adventures, many more adventures were embarked upon by other young men, and the ignorant, carefree people were ever willing to give up their treasured maidens to unscrupulous greedy foreigners.

Eventually, the wealth of Mr. T and his people increased through the exploitation of these people, whose fortunes were significantly depleted. The fools never recovered to this day. As more maidens were married off this way, their own young men had no maidens to marry and their economy collapsed.

*   *   *

There was a sudden movement of the earth around Uncle Sam's house and a photo frame on the wall fell and smashed on the floor scattering broken glass everywhere. Uncle Sam was jolted to reality while still reflecting on the story Pa Ikedi had told the children.

The similarity of the experience between the towns' encounters in Pa Ikedi's story and the encounter between the Europeans and their colonized territories in Africa and America struck Uncle Sam with full force. He shuddered at this sudden realization.

"Is that how we shall end as Africans?" he asked in total disappointment.

RELIGIOUS RITES

"Have I told you about the *Ebi* rituals?" the old man asked the children. One of them had asked to know how *Ebi* was worshipped at one of their previous story-telling sessions.

"The ancestor cult, or *Ebi*, keeps ancestral protection and benevolence flowing; it also puts those who are uninitiated into contact with the shades of the dead. The *Ebi* maintains the ancestral lineage and teaches people the traditional values. Sometimes they must use ritual gestures because the dead have two wayward tendencies: they either become preoccupied with their own affairs in the land of the dead, or they come into the land of the living, manifesting themselves in uncontrolled ways.

"The dead should naturally feel a protective benevolence toward the living," Pa Ikedi said. "But, the dead might become jealous of the living, resenting those who hurried them on their way to the grave, afflicting the living with diseases or even killing them by calling them to the land of the dead.

"These rituals, as I've witnessed, are often administered to young men who need ancestral surveillance because of marriage and its responsibilities. They might choose initiation because of a spell of misfortunes, but it's important as the marriage engagement is a promise to have children for the propagation of the family; all the parties involved must come to terms with the uniqueness of a relationship that ties two or more families together.

"Initiation might occur even though there is no new skull available to contribute to the reliquary, a container for holy relics. But often enough an influential 'father' would have died not long before, and the young initiate is brought into the cult together with the respected relic, which guarantees his domestic well-being.

"The initiation involves falling 'dead,' falling senseless under the influence of the rasped root bark of the bush, which affects the central nervous system. Under the influence of this root bark, the initiate becomes possessed of the ancestral spirit. He is physically 'dead' because he is oblivious to his immediate environment and starts having vivid interactions with the ancestral spirit that guides his family unit. It may seem unbelievable but it is surely real. The initiation confers honor and prestige on the male head of the family so he can walk tall with family pride.

"Before the initiation, a forest enclosure is prepared, with a chamber in front and a hidden chamber in the back. The skulls are lined up on a platform of banana trunks in the middle chamber.

"As many as three or four people might participate together with their reliquaries. Meanwhile in the village, the initiate sits down on a banana tree trunk in the courtyard. He must have fasted and had no sexual contact for at least four days before the initiation rite. As he eats the *agba* root, villagers dance around him to the accompaniment of drums, xylophones and harps. They bend over him and shout in his ears. These rhythmical activities mesmerize him as much as the drug itself. The songs are like funeral songs, for they all anticipate the 'death' of the initiate.

"Then traditional singers sing a song that goes like this." And Pa Ikedi began to sing.

Oh father, when you abandon the earth,
Your spirit passes to the other side.
Oh father, why do you leave the earth?
The sky clears but the eyes darken.
The water drops from the tree.
The hollow seed shells fall.
Look at the "house" which was our father.
Gather the medicinal herbs;
Sprinkle them to the right side and to the left side.
A man now sees hidden things.

"What does the song mean?" a child asked.

"It is a funeral song to appease the dead. The water dropping from the trees is an allusion to the misty dawn in the humid forest when the spirits are most actively returning to their home.

"It is just like the songs you sing when someone dies in your church these days. There is also spirit departure: the flight of a large bird (or the soul) out of the tree (or the body) where it has been perched all through the person's lifetime.

"Can I continue?" Pa Ikedi asked, feeling happy that these story-telling sessions were nurturing the children's intellect.

"Yes, you can!" the children said in chorus.

"The initiate is laid on a mat, and his face is washed with an infusion of medicinal herbs. lf they think he ate too much of the *agba* root, a scourge of branches is prepared and dipped into a basin hollowed in the earth and lined with leaves. The initiate is gently whipped on his body until he is revived. This moment is always feared, for it is said that some may die, taken permanently by the ancestors to the land of the dead never to return; perhaps they are not welcomed by the ancestors and left to wander as malevolent shades among the forces of nature." Pa Ikedi paused; the children looked confused.

"Why do they beat the man?" one child asked.

"To become a man is not a day's job my child. You must have a strong influence from *Nnne Oha* (wise woman); then you have to show that you are strong and can be responsible enough to build a home. If your mother and father are not strong, they can't take care of you," the old man said with assertion.

The children nodded in agreement for, at that moment, each remembered how tirelessly their parents, especially their fathers, worked to provide for them and the entire family. The story had struck a familiar chord in their lives, and they were getting more and more interested. Their whole attention was focused on the revered old man sitting in their midst entertaining them.

"After this flogging, the villagers withdraw briefly to give the initiate and the priest a few moments to rest. Then they wait anxiously for the sound of the forest drum. It tells them whether the initiate has recovered his life or not."

"What if the drum doesn't sound?" a child asked.

"Then the shame is on his family, for the non-awakening of an initiate is interpreted as a lack of coordination between the living members of the family and their ancestral forebears.

"Once the drum sounds and the candidate recovers, he sings a song of passage, which goes like this."

I have finished disposing my heart well.
He has well-disposed it.
He has finished preparing himself.
Look, I am humbled and brought low.
Look, I am no longer the hard heart.
Look, we are humbled.
Look, no hard heart.

When Pa Ikedi was asked why it was necessary for the initiate to eat concoctions and die, he responded by saying, "The ancestors, being dead and on the other side, can accomplish the miracles of things unseen. Men who join the ancestral cult should die and know something of what it means to 'eat with the dead.' They should have their skulls opened so that they can stand between the life of the village and the memory of the ancestors.

"When the cult uses the word 'die,' it doesn't mean it's irreversible, that you won't wake up again. The body only stops as if dead because it consumes the concoctions. In the initiation ceremony, the initiate does not lose his life. He makes only half the trip to the land of the dead. But having made that, he can thereafter continue to make contact with the ancestors.

"In the evening after the ceremony, the initiate receives signs from the ancestors. The newly initiated sleep with the bark barrel containing the skulls at the head of their beds. The cult members anxiously question the initiate the next morning: 'Did you dream the death of someone? Did you dream you were wandering cold and alone in the forest? Did you dream of killing an animal, of a marriage festival, of eating in the council house?'"

"What happens after that?" a child asked.

"You're right. That's not the end of the *Ebi* ritual," said Pa Ikedi, nodding. "While the initiate recovers in the front chamber of the forest, the members keep busy refortifying the skulls. A sheep and a chicken are sacrificed, and their blood is poured into another basin of banana leaves in which the bark of several powerful and medicinal trees, the head of a viper and boiling water are all mixed. The skulls are washed in this mixture and set on the banana trunk platform in a row. The new skull, if present, is washed last and placed in front of the others. The cult members begin to dance in circles before the skulls and around them. Occasionally they pick them up and dance with them held low over the ground.

"The initiate, now revived, is taken down to the stream to be washed thoroughly but carefully. It is forbidden to appear before the *Ebi* elders covered with dirt and perspiration. When the initiate is thoroughly clean, the *Obu Ofo*, who is usually the eldest member and therefore the head of the cult, applies the red *padouk* powder to one side – the left side – of the new initiate's body and raffia palm oil to his other side. The palm oil signifies cleanliness, and the padouk powder, joyfulness at his recovery. These are the same substances used to clean the reliquary figure.

"In the hidden chamber, the skulls are packed into barrels and the members, in the company of the initiate, dance into the village square holding the reliquaries in their hands. Once again they sing, 'Fathers have come ...' The barrels are taken to their respective chambers, except for the family barrel of the latest initiate; it is placed at the head of his bed. The medicine child stares down on him. He is prepared for his dreams and for an ancestral message. And finally, the elder of his clan or household offers a benediction before the reliquary.

"On the second day of the festival, the initiate is shown the skulls of the ancestors, since he has graduated from his initial state of ignorance to a new state as the possessor of unique, secret knowledge. When his dreams have been interpreted, he is taken once again to the forest clearing. The reliquaries will already be brought out and the skulls set in their rows but screened from view by a curtain. Before the skulls are shown, the reliquary figures appear over the barrier in the clearing, while voices from behind the scene menacingly demand the initiate's name, his genealogy and what he dreamed.

"At this point," said the old man, "a mirror is placed before him on the ground. He is told to stare into it. The mirror is then gradually shifted so that the skulls on the banana trunk come into view behind the parted barrier. The *Obu Ofo* directs the initiate to stand before the raffia curtain, which is lifted to reveal the skulls. The main objective is to startle the initiate with the 'miracle of the craniums.'

"The initiate is then questioned in the following way.

'And this, what is it called?' a voice asks the new initiate.
'I do not know,' he answers.
'I will teach you. Be attentive.'
'I am attentive,' the new initiate responds, holding his ears in a gesture of attentiveness.
'This thing was in the past. It is and it will be,' the voice begins.

"And so lessons will follow. In this way the instruction of the initiate begins with the family identity of the various skulls. And preparation is made for the recitation of the genealogy of the skulls.

This is your grandfather. You will work together and you will care for each other. When you go on a journey, bid him farewell and ask his blessing. When you kill an antelope, give him the best part; do not let the woman touch it. Keep him clean. Come to him from time to time and wash him.

"After this, the initiate makes the following vows to his Father.

You, Father, who knows not death,
Who rests impervious to death,
You live on, knowing life no longer as we mortals do.
You feel no cold, no sleepiness
Because you remain awake to guard us all.
Your people have come to you.
Hear us, as we are children
Who know nothing except what you teach.
Hear us and guide us well to fullness.
They assemble themselves,
Your group, your heritage, your legacy;
Give to us your capacity. Your power, Father.
Remain to share with the people your spirit.
You, Father, you do not know death as we mortals do.
You, Father of our clan, the great man,
Who gave all life.

"It is in this way," said Pa Ikedi, "that our lifecycle as a people rolls on. The African society believes that the existences of the dead, the living and the unborn are intertwined. None live their fulfillment without the other. The ancestors are the guardian spirits of the clan. The living are judged by virtue of their actions in how they maintain and spread the values of the clan. The ancestors' interaction with the living assures that norms and values are sustained. The arrival of new birth carries with it the blessing of the reincarnated spirits of the good ancestors.

"The *Ebi* rituals guarantee a constant process for the living to gauge their lives and fulfill their destinies. The initiation rites introduce the young initiate into the world of the elders so they can participate in the decision-making process of the clan. The initiate is welcomed to adulthood."

6 EBI MOVES THROUGH THE SEA

"Wars, destruction, burnt huts, exposed brains from machete cuts, arms and fingers dancing on the ground, and blood on the faces of the invaders as helpless victims begged for their most precious possessions: their lives.

"They came from different tribes and lands," Pa Ikedi said. "They spoke different languages – Portuguese and Bini, German and Igbo, English and Mende, Spanish and Ashanti and so on. They were fueled by ambition, adventure and power; others were bought and sold like livestock. Together, they journeyed through the sea.

"Many people today live in denial. They say, 'My father or grandfather did not do it,' but today, it is part of our story. In today's world, to be black means to be a slave and to be white means to be a slave master. This is the reality today.

"Squeezed into the cramped hold of a large boat, bound in chains, several of our men and women were taken captive against their own will." Pa Ikedi scanned the room, taking a few moments to look at the faces of the children gathered around him. The level of attention he devoted to scanning the room showed he was taking notice of the children's attendance at the storytelling sessions. "Where is Ifesi?" Pa Ikedi asked, cutting short his narrative.

"Oh, he has not come," one of the children answered.

"His mom said he was ill," a boy added.

The room was silent as Pa Ikedi rounded off his scrutiny before continuing his story.

* * *

Baku, was one of the greatest warriors in the land. He was recently initiated into the *Ebi* cult, having just attained the age. His father spent so much for him to join the cult, which carried with it for any young man the mark of age allowing him to move around with respect and dignity, knowing he had dedicated himself to the defense of his society.

Baku was considered because of his large chest and height, two things that were essential for a warrior.

One day, vandals from neighboring villages invaded our village in a surprise attack. Since it was forbidden for our people to fight war during the *Ebi* festival, there was little our people could do as all the warriors were busy appeasing the gods. What happened changed the history of our people forever.

Baku was kidnapped during his seclusion period by some fierce-looking men, who appeared stronger than he was. He tried to escape, but his strength failed him. Perhaps he had yet to recover from the seemingly unending flogging that was the hallmark of the *Ebi* ritual.

He was caught and tied like a goat for days by his abductors. Other captives joined him. His two sisters, Bangi and Mungi, were tied and left bare-chested; their warrior princess breasts that stood like cherries had no protection. Baku had thought he would collect so much money, as the eldest son in the family, from boys brave enough to dare ask her warrior sisters hand in marriage. Now, he did not know how that would turn out.

For several days that seemed like an eternity, about twenty-four people were tied up by their captors; they were given very little food. On one of those days, Baku saw the head of their captors' clan warriors, Gbendi, talking with a white man. He did not know what they were saying. But he heard him say "tomorrow" in their language.

"Are we going to be freed tomorrow?" he thought. "Gbendi cannot be so nice. His clan maintains a bitter rivalry with ours. Their people are forbidden from marrying from our clan." He remembered his father telling him once to be careful of the Bara people. "They are man-eaters," his father had told him.

One thing he knew for sure was that their village was more urbanized than the Bara. They had to join his village in trading. The routes to Bara passed through the *Ebi* clan. The river that supplied Bara people water for drinking and fishing was the great Osin River. Bara people had fought his people in the past because of the Osin River but were defeated. To his people, Osin was more than just a river; it was the home of the goddess, Osin. She was believed to protect her people from disease, famine and poverty. In war, Osin, when invoked, will defend her people.

The sun set and there was still no sign of any freedom in sight. Baku was defenseless against six armed, fierce-looking Bara warriors. Even if he could make any attempt, his hands and legs would be at the mercy of the ropes!

"We move now," the leader of the Bara said. Baku did not know his name, but with the way the Bara warriors obeyed his command, Baku knew he must be a high-ranking general.

The ropes around them were carefully tied to bamboo sticks and they were made to walk in single file; each within the bamboo pack knew they were at the mercy of one other. If one of them fell or walked slowly, the entire column would be flogged to move. This required more strength from each member.

Throughout the journey, Baku saw some of his clansmen die; the coach would just cut off the dead person from the column and leave the body for wild animals. In some cases, if a captive was close to death from exhaustion, the coach just threw them off from the column or stabbed them till they bled to death. One of the warrior guards actually gloated after performing this act of death during their journey to the large boat, shouting, "Dead men can't bite!"

However, Baku knew after his initiation into the *Ebi* cult that dead men could and do indeed bite. He was surprised and wondered where this Bara warrior had learned it. The white-skinned man must have taught him that.

As they got to the seashore, Baku saw a large boat. He had never seen such a thing since he was born. He had never believed a boat could be bigger than several huts. He had also never seen a boat made of iron.

It soon started raining. One very brave woman delivered herself of a baby while still in chains. The coaches were busy trying to get all their captives into the large boat on the shore.

"Move in!" one of the commanders commanded. Pandemonium set in as the coaches flogged their captives into the large boat. Like yams in a barn, the captives lay on top of one another in the large boat.

Baku realized the boat must have swallowed up his whole village. They must have been up to five hundred of them in that space feeling the cold. The smell of vomit, feces, urine and sweat contaminated the air. The only source of light was through the small holes in the boat that opened to the sky. And still, none of the captives could reach it. Their chains prevented them from moving about.

"*Ebi,* come and save your child," Baku prayed but there was no response. By this time, they had spent days in the boat.

"I must get back home," Baku said.

"How can you?" a fellow captive from one of the neighboring towns asked.

"I don't know. But I know I will fight my way back home. I am a warrior."

"So how did you get here if you are a warrior?" a captive who was lying down two human spaces to his right asked. "Why couldn't you fight when you were caught? Why didn't you tell the Bara that you are a warrior when they were loading you into this ship? Where was your warrior strength when they invaded your village? Please say something else."

"If you have decided to be a slave," Baku said, "good for you. For me, I am a warrior and I am trained to fight. If I die, so be it."

The light from the holes in the boat showed them if it was day or night. Baku saw something metal that looked like what his father used for traps. With his hands in chains, he could not do anything to get to it. He knew the coaches would soon come and order them out to get fresh air as they had done since they mounted the boat. As he passed by, Baku picked up the metal and kept it in the sack cloth he used as clothes.

Once back in the belly of the boat, Baku used the metal to slowly cut off his chains. After a few minutes, it broke. He opened his eyes wide to make sure he was not dreaming. His fellow captives wanted to get out of their chains too. One by one, Baku and the initial captives he released helped to get the chains off the hands and feet of all the captives.

That same night, they found the sailors' tools, machetes, guns and other fighting items. The captives seized them all and were fully ready for battle. In number, they were greater; Baku had learned as a warrior that numbers posed an advantage in war. They had to stage an attack immediately or lose the element of surprise.

One of the female cooks informed the captives that the crew had taken excessive alcohol that night. One by one, they moved out of the belly of the ship, holding cutlasses, knives, guns, swords, nails and other weapons of death. And then, Baku and his gang came face to face with their captors. The Europeans reached for their guns and the stage was set for a bloody fight.

7. THE SACRILEGE

Pa Ikedi sat with his head bent low. His white hairs spoke eloquently of the many sunrises and sunsets they had seen.

"Hmmmm," he sighed.

"It seems your heart is heavy papa," one of his listeners said. He was a young boy of about twelve.

"Yes, my son," he said.

"They descended on our land, destroyed our crops, burned our houses, killed our children and desecrated our communities all in a time of chaos," Pa Ikedi said as he began his story.

"Rampaging fires destroyed our forests; the ocean went wild in warning. The heavens seemed to have forgotten how to make rain." He covered his face as though he wanted to cry. Since it was a taboo for the tears of an old man to be seen by children, his audience simply bent their heads. One of them, Chidi, went close to Pa Ikedi and gently wiped and cleansed his eyes.

"Pregnant women gave birth to goats, rather than babies," Pa Ikedi continued. "Mud holes dried, and the ground became hardened. We planted, but there was no increase; they turned to stone. The gods didn't accept our seeds even in planting seasons. There was no harvest.

"Mothers went mad seeing their babies die of hunger. Fights broke out among our people; everyone wanted to blame someone or something for their predicament.

"The elders of the land gathered in desperation for a solution but found none. And the suffering continued.

"One day, a woman appeared in our midst from a distant land. She looked largely unkempt, looking like the madwoman in the Ajape market. Her hair was scattered; her clothes, half-torn. Stranger still, she had two leopards moving with her."

"Who's this woman?" someone from the audience asked.

"It turned out that she was a wise woman. She was not mad as we earlier thought. After looking upon our chaotic land, she demanded to see our king.

"She told us that a sacrilege committed by our fathers was the reason for our suffering. We must worship, as she did, to reverse the curse on our land."

"How did she worship?" a child asked.

"That is a good question," said Pa Ikedi. "I will tell you the story of Waka, for that was the name of the wise woman, told to our elders in the council."

* * *

A long time ago, there once lived a powerful priest who was the guardian of the sacred temple at Jiga, the centre of the earth.

The name of this priest was Gole. He communicated with the gods on behalf of the people. He spoke directly to the gods. They heard his voice, and he heard them.

This temple was home to a lot of people seeking solutions to personal and family problems. People came from near and far to worship at the temple in Jiga.

Our ancestors were made to march for days on foot before they could reach the centre of the earth at Jiga. A prophecy said they would see an Iroko tree, and at that point they would meet the gods.

This temple existed for several centuries and had seen many priests come and go. Bagba, the fourteenth priest to serve the temple, became unusually famous throughout the lands. He had all the powers of the previous priests, but he also had one the previous ones did not have – he got angry very easily.

Because of his bad temper, he had running battles with the palace. He issued curses, using his potent totems against those who had the minutest disagreement with him.

Bagba's father, who previously served as priest, lived as long as anyone could remember. He was loved by all. No one recalled him ever issuing any curse, using the totems against the people. The totems were powerful and were only to be used on very rare or special occasions and not on those who disagreed with the priest.

One story about Bagba painted him as a very crooked person indeed. Before he became the priest, he once hired a close friend of his to help lead his caravan of porters to a neighboring village. When they arrived at the village, he went secretly to some slave traders and offered to sell his friend to them as a slave. The bargain was struck, Bagba received payment, and the slave traders grabbed his friend and bound and gagged him for the journey through the villages to the coast where they would sell him to slave ships. Fortunately for the poor man, village police officials came to the scene, released him and arrested Bagba. Then they brought Bagba before the palace, and the village head had him seriously punished.

Many years later, Bagba became priest, and one of the police officers who caught him during the inglorious slave trade became king. Bagba saw his opportunity to get his pound of flesh for the previous humiliation.

Now, using the totem against a sitting king by a priest was a horrible thing to even think of. Still, Bagba went ahead and issued the threat, and the battle for supremacy arose between the priest and the palace.

Embarrassed by the priest's recent public denigration of the king and the palace, the king had had enough. Either the king or the priest must vacate the village.

The council of elders met one night and decided the chief priest must leave the village within three days. The palace messenger was sent to deliver this message to him.

The reaction of the priest was to shock the palace. He sent the messenger back to the palace to say that it was the king who must leave the village and not the other way round.

"This temple was here before the palace," Bagba said.

On the third day, the council of elders decided to invite the army to enforce their earlier decision. The entire village, in support of the king, matched towards the temple to enforce the king's orders. The priest had little choice. He went to the Orija mountain that morning with his totems, where he issued the following words:

"Oh, ye spirits of my ancestors who have served *Ebi*, I call you out today. Your people have turned against you and your spirit by banishing me, your chief defender, from them. You spirits were here before the palace was established. From today, you spirits of our land must rise to defend yourselves from these ambitious people who know no respect.

"They shall remain tormented and disunited. They shall be forcefully and bloodily moved from the village to other lands. They shall be tormented in the strange lands they will subsequently find themselves in.

"The earth shall torment them anywhere they move. The seas shall swallow them, including those who take them captive. Violence from the deepest parts of the earth shall rise to consume them. Their seeds shall never lead to increase. The earth shall not respond to their calls.

"Come to my aid, O ye spirits, and answer thine own son. So shall it be."

After saying these words from the top of the mountain, he took some pills out of his small bag and swallowed them, and in a few minutes, he chanted, "I've made myself the sacrificial item for this solemn offering," and gave up the ghost. And nobody heard anything of Bagba, the priest from the village, ever again.

✳ ✳ ✳

Pa Ikedi continued his story about the slave ship. "Our ancestors were chained together in rows. They were made to march for days on foot with empty bellies. The white slave traders came to choose and buy their goods – human beings at the point of no return."

"That's horrible," one of the listeners said.

"Before they were taken away from the village to begin the long march towards the shore," Pa Ikedi said, "each captive was made to circle the Iroko tree seven times to erase the memory of their lands.

"The captives left everything behind, but the curse for desecration of their lands issued decades before still followed them wherever they were taken.

"Because the only thing the captives could take with them was the curse, they spread it to other lands and seas as they were transported. The curse was so potent because it was issued at the point of death, because Bagba made himself a sacrificial item by taking his own life.

"Today," Pa Ikedi said, "the temple has largely been forgotten. But even though most of it was destroyed during the slave raids and wars that followed immediately after the priest passed on, there are a few still dedicated to worshipping there.

"Tutu is the name of its current priest, and he is searching for a successor. He is desperately looking for someone to pass on his secret knowledge.

"I visited what remains of this temple a few years ago to see things for myself. That was how I came to know about this; Tutu does not want the secret to die with him."

8: THE GODS ARE SPEAKING

Uncle Sam had been trying to make sense of Pa Ikedi's stories for some days running. He had recently bought a book called *God is Wicked*, written by American atheist Garry Zeid, who blamed God for allowing all natural disasters to happen in the world. Uncle Sam did not understand why anyone would blame God for everything bad that happened in the world and not give him credit for the positive developments in the world.

There is a quote that Uncle Sam had read that says: "Florida has its hurricanes; California, its earthquakes." The saying made it sound as if it was an obvious insight, but there was nothing natural about disasters, as if the geographies were to blame. The land wasn't born risky. It was built that way.

But in Florida, land was given away and natural resources were sold to private interests. Developers were given hefty subsidies to build on barrier islands and other places that were prone to flooding. This sowed the seed of future destruction as businessmen denied there was any risks involved or blamed nature or God when disaster occurred. Florida had a very shadowy history when it came to natural disasters.

Miami Beach was originally just a thin spit of sand about two hundred feet wide, with a low ridge of dunes running down it. By the bay, weeds gave way to a tangled swamp of red mangroves, which had dense roots and stems. But a swamp of mangroves that's buzzing with mosquitoes and sand flies wasn't the kind of tropical paradise that would attract tourists; what followed was years of denial about the environment for the sake of development with more hotels and suburban sprawl.

"Why," Uncle Sam asked himself, "were Florida, New York and other areas around the coast some of the worst hit by hurricanes?"

The most recent, Hurricane Irma, kept coming to mind. He remembered Pa Ikedi once saying such things were not natural. "If such destruction happens in our time, we know the gods are speaking."

"So, what are the gods saying this time?" Uncle Sam wondered.

He thought of the refrain "Americans don't believe in the African voodoo."

"How then," Uncle Sam asked, "can they appease the gods they don't believe in?"

In one of his discussions with Pa Ikedi, the old man had told him, "You don't need to believe in our gods. They are always there whether you believe them or not.

"Our gods are powerful. If you defile them, they will act and will speak to you in the way you will understand. In some cases, they can cause many months of rains. In other cases, they can hold the rains from falling for years as it happened in Owerri Nkworji town when they offended the gods. They can also use fire.

"You people who know too many books think our gods are dead. You were told of one God who is 'living' and therefore abandoned the gods our ancestors had worshipped for generations before the white man set foot on our soil.

"Just think about it," Pa Ikedi said. "In the past, when you defied the land, you offended *Isi Ala*, the god of the earth. Isn't it right? If you stole a yam, it was an offence against *Ala*, the land. In that case, the offender was made to confess their sins against the land, or the god of the earth would punish them. Nobody wanted to be punished by the gods because they knew how powerful the gods were.

"I remember years ago when I was a little boy, a young man went onto someone's land and stole his harvest. Even though someone saw him steal the harvest, the young man denied it vehemently. It is a shameful thing to steal. It was considered a crime to steal anything in the community. A thief was a disgrace to his relatives and his entire family.

"The owner of the harvest appealed to the priest for help, and the priest performed the necessary rituals to detect the thief and recover the stolen property. The priest used sacrificial items, cajoling and pleading for the suspect to come forward and confess; if the thief did, the rites would be halted and the punishment would be less.

"The priest performed some libations so the thief could be revealed publicly by the gods or be made to confess publicly and return the stolen property where it could be seen by the people. The divine power of the gods could make the thief suffer physically or mentally. However, the thief did not confess and the rites were effectively concluded. After a few days, the unimaginable happened.

"The young man became subjected to a combination of prolonged torture, illness, paralysis and partial blindness, to the point that diviners were consulted to unravel the cause of his misfortunes. When it was discovered that his misfortunes came about because he had been stealing, the stolen goods had to be returned and a sacrifice had to offered in atonement.

"Stealing is not only abominable and condemnable; it is also a religious offence punishable by the gods," Pa Ikedi said. "The great oracle Odu Ogbe-Ala warns against stealing:

If the earthly king does not see you,

The heavenly king is looking at you.

Thus declares the oracle to the one who steals

Under the cover of darkness,

Who says that the earthly king does not see him.

God sees the thief and will surely punish him.

"Seeing, here," Pa Ikedi said, "does not mean merely looking, but seeing for punishment."

"What if you stole from the community?" Uncle Sam asked.

"I just told you what would happen if you stole from just one person. What do you think would happen if you stole from a whole community?" Pa Ikedi countered. "That is a recipe for disaster. You cannot steal from a community and have peace.

"Stealing goods that belong to an entire community is bad, but taking human beings is worse."

"What do you mean?" Uncle Sam asked uneasily.

"Take a look at all the routes our people were taken through to the white man's land. You will notice those are the places our gods also journeyed through with them," Pa Ikedi answered.

Uncle Sam did not understand what Pa Ikedi meant, but undoubtedly something strange was building up in his mind, which he could not readily fathom.

"What did they call that thing that was destroying their houses?" Pa Ikedi asked.

"Hurricane Irma, sir," Uncle Sam said with alarm.

66

"I don't know what that means," Pa Ikedi responded with a frown.

"A hurricane," Uncle Sam said, "is a large, swirling storm that's faster than a cheetah. They named Hurricane Irma after a woman, and it was extremely powerful and catastrophic, the strongest storm on record in the Atlantic. They say it started in Cape Verde in West Africa, building up powerful force as it moved across the Atlantic, moving like a heavy fire from under the ocean and striking the land with great speed and terrible destructive force."

"So it came from West Africa and moved like lightning to strike the nearest land?"

"You are right, sir."

"Let me ask you some questions," Pa Ikedi said.

"Go on, sir," Uncle Sam replied, priming his ears.

"Who were the people the white man took as slaves?"

"The black people, sir."

"Where were the black people from?"

"From West Africa, sir."

"Where did you say this thing that destroys the white man's land today came from?"

"West Africa, sir."

"And you said West Africa is the land of the black man, right?"

"Yes, sir."

"Then use your tongue to count your teeth, Sam."

"What are you insinuating, papa? Are you saying the slaves the white men took from our land haunt them today?" Uncle Sam asked, perplexed.

"Listen, Sam," Pa Ikedi said in a solemn voice that betrayed no emotions. "In Igbo land, there is a god called Amadi Oha; he's the god of thunder. He can strike those who offend him from a great distance and at short notice." Pa Ikedi adjusted on his seat to make himself more comfortable. "Let me tell you about Amadi Oha."

*   *   *

The Igbo people believe that Amuma Igwe, or lightning, associated with Amadi Oha is a sign of impending doom or evil from the gods, and they also believe it has a track. The natives always avoid those tracks to be on the safe side. They also believe that Egbe Elu-Igwe, or thunder, is the messenger of Amadi Oha.

Amuma Igwe is sent to destroy evildoers, or the houses and trees in which evil things are hidden or buried, such as poison and other negative concoctions that are meant to harm others. There are cases where evil men and women are struck to death by lightning as they returned from imparting some dangerous charm and poison to kill their neighbor, relative or friend because of disputed land or property.

Worshippers of Amadi Oha say the following prayers to appease him:

Nna Amadi Oha, god of our forefathers and foremothers,

we come before you with clear consciences, unburdened hearts and clean hands.

We pray that you help us to remember that good judgment and good character are more valuable than any amount of money or power, and that with your help, we can work to develop both.

We humbly ask that we may never turn a blind eye to injustice, for we know that injustice anywhere is a threat to justice everywhere.

May we work to right what has been wronged and fix what has been spoiled.

✳   ✳   ✳

"Did I hear you say that Amuma Igwe moves like lightning?" asked Uncle Sam.

"Yes," Pa Ikedi said. "When the land is bleeding like this, it means the gods are speaking!"

Uncle Sam was confounded and perplexed. How could a geographical phenomenon such as destructive wind action in Florida be connected to the transatlantic slave trade that took place centuries ago? But Pa Ikedi's connections sounded so clear and related. These fundamental issues disturbed his peace and sent his spirit raging.

"How can that be? It's not possible. It's unimaginable," he muttered under his breath because, for him, there was no connection between these seemingly disparate entities. "But, the fierce winds that gave rise to Hurricane Irma did originate in West Africa and they did travel the same route as the slaves who were forcefully taken to the Americas.

"That's impossible!" he finally uttered; he felt truly startled by the connection and the implication.

THE TOTEMS

Pa Ikedi felt it necessary to tell a story of the tortoise and the birds all over again. The story was about how the tortoise came up with a shell that was pieced together rather than being smooth. The children enjoyed it when it was first told but not all of them were present that first day.

On this night, Chinedu and Uncle Sam sat back to enjoy Pa Ikedi's stories with the children. Since the audience now included full-grown adults, Pa Ikedi decided to change his mind. Stories like that were too low-rated for adults.

Pa Ikedi decided to tell some more mature stories so that the children could also know more about who they were, their origin and the ways of their ancestors.

Since his last discussion with Pa Ikedi, Uncle Sam had not recovered from his shock and disbelief that the gods of Africa followed slaves to the white man's land to torment the white man. He was conflicted about the story, and his dilemma was enormous. As a literary icon, how could he relate this incredible connection between African beliefs and the natural phenomena in America to his friends or to the outside world without being ridiculed?

"Everyone will think I'm mad," he said to himself.

"No one will think you are mad my son," Pa Ikedi said, overhearing him. "You obviously do not understand what I am saying."

"Then make me understand, papa."

"If I tell you, you won't understand. But if you want to know more, I will take you somewhere."

"Where is that?"

"The temple in Jiga."

"Where is that located?"

"Ask fewer questions. I will take you there when you are ready."

"Let's go next week. I want to find out a lot of things."

"You will get all the answers you seek. But I don't have all the answers here with me. As an old man, I cannot tell you what I don't know."

Pa Ikedi yawned. He looked exhausted. Recently Uncle Sam had paid huge medical bills to get him discharged from the hospital. His age was taking a toll on his health. "If I join my ancestors at my age," Pa Ikedi had once told Sam as he ate a breakfast of pap, or corn pudding, while at Saint Jude's Catholic Hospital, "there will be no panic because I have done enough for myself and for my society on this earth."

He was suffering from diabetes. If not for the fact that Pa Ikedi had initially been unconscious, he would never have allowed them take him to the "white man's *juju* centre" where "white chalk is given as medicine and needle is used to pierce veins," as Pa Ikedi would say. That it was a Catholic Hospital, again, would have been another reason for Pa Ikedi to object. He would have insisted that "some Reverend sisters will come wearing their charms on their necks holding one on their hands and telling somebody that it is 'Jesus that healed you.'"

Because he was advised to start sleeping early and take his drugs, Uncle Sam knew Pa Ikedi would follow none of the advice. It was already past eight o'clock, and Pa Ikedi was still with the children outside. Since papa was yawning, Uncle Sam sent the children to their homes for the night.

* * *

The bus conductor kept shouting "Momuregbo! Momuregbo!" at the top of his voice. The motor park was as noisy as when Uncle Sam knew it some years ago, before he could afford his own car. This time, he had to join a commercial bus to Momuregbo because he was not familiar with the route they were to use and therefore could not drive his own car.

Meanwhile, Pa Ikedi seemed to have lost memories of the routes since he was last there decades ago; he had contemplated it for some time but could not reconstruct the direction in his mind. Giving up the attempt, Pa Ikedi found consolation in the fact that, if worse came to worst, he would certainly remember the right names to call for easier identification. One thing was clear – he knew for sure that when they got to Momuregbo, he could always get the directions to the temple at Jiga.

The dirty-looking bus conductor kept screaming for passengers to join his bus. It was 6:30 on a Saturday morning, so many people were not traveling that day. The motor park was kept busy by buses dropping off their passengers traveling to the city, probably to attend some social events or visit their loved ones for the weekend.

Momuregbo was about a six hour drive; Uncle Sam knew he could not drive for that long without fatigue. Pa Ikedi himself was used to traveling such long distances. His recently declining health notwithstanding, Pa Ikedi knew that patience and endurance would get them to the temple at Jiga.

"You will have to shift, madam. It's four on a seat," the bus conductor said to a female passenger as he adjusted the passengers' luggage at the back of the bus.

"This heavy woman should pay for two persons, na. Na, so your husband dey carry you?" the bus conductor said in response to comments from a voluminous female passenger who was feeling inconvenienced by this constant call of "madam shift, madam shift." The woman frowned initially, but knowing the nature of bus conductors, felt it was better to rise above the tantrums and throw back the banter to the bus conductor.

"Na, you know wetin de spoil your mind. You no go face your work. Whether my husband complained for you?" the woman asked, and everyone in the bus laughed.

"Some men de like-am extra large," one man said. "Some like medium size. Some like-am lepa. It is a matter of choice." The passengers again roared with laughter.

"Extra large or *orobo* means you chop better food. If you no get money, you no go fit carry *orobo* like me," the fat woman said.

"But why you no fit pay for two seats na or carry drop?" the bus conductor asked her.

"That one na your business. Na talk you wan talk. If to say I take drop, you for get this blessing of seeing me today?" the woman added.

Again, the passengers laughed.

"Momuregbo, one seat!" the conductor shouted again as he began collecting money from the passengers, a short stub of a Rothmans cigarette in his mouth.

It was time for the bus to move but the driver was nowhere to be found. His bus conductor ran to look for him after settling the park officials. In a short while, he was back with the driver who looked older than his age and was holding a small bottle of Chelsea gin.

"Sorry, my people. I have been driving for the past thirty-something years. I just went to take my own fuel just like I am going to fuel this bus as we head for Momuregbo."

After seeing the driver with the bottle, many of the passengers didn't know whether to demand a refund from the bus conductor or continue with the journey.

"My *oga* is a professional driver," the conductor said excitedly, having sensed the misgivings in some passengers. "He don drive govonor, sinato, minster and top people for this we country. So no worry yourself, passengers. We go reach Momuregbo. Somebody give us prayers. Pilot, fire on!"

The driver took another sip from the bottle of Chelsea gin and started the engine. "My people make una no worry. Person no be firewood," he said calmly.

"Our Father in Heaven," a passenger started to pray, "lead us safely to our various destinations. We pray for the driver to see clearly as he drives us in the course of this journey. O God, come and take over this journey from the driver. We all entered this bus through the door; please, don't let us all come out through the window."

The passengers all shouted, "Amen!"

"O God," he continued praying, "let us not be bathed in our own blood."

The passengers shouted, "Amen!"

"Let us get to our various destinations in one piece and in peace, and don't let those we didn't inform of our journeys today know where we went. Let us all meet our relatives in our different homes in peace; in Jesus's name I have prayed."

And the other passengers shouted, "Amen!"

The bus was already gathering speed on the highway by the time the prayer was concluded.

✳ ✳ ✳

When the bus arrived in Momuregbo, it was two o'clock in the afternoon. Pa Ikedi and Uncle Sam started navigating their way towards the temple. It was situated deep in the jungle and the cars could not be driven on the roads. All the buses at the parks complained about the danger of plying that route.

"If your bus gets stuck in the muddy road, just forget about your vehicle. It's gone forever," a bus owner at the park said. "The bad spirit on that road is the reason government no fit do the road."

Legend had it that a prominent politician who wanted to construct the road to the temple died a few days after the work started. It was also said that most of the workers who went to dig the route to the temple died of various diseases. Since then, many who visited the temple did so either by passing through the Imo River by boat or trekking long distances to reach the temple. Pa Ikedi and Uncle Sam opted for the former. For this, they needed a guide!

"This is the most dangerous route on earth, so you have to be very careful and watch your steps," their guide, Okoro, a middle-aged man, warned. "There are so many things that can kill anybody of unclean mind in this jungle. It's like walking in the land of the dead," he stressed.

Uncle Sam looked at Okoro's face in horror, wondering why he volunteered in the first place to leave the comfort of his large home in the city in search of a forgotten temple. But Pa Ikedi looked unperturbed. He had undertaken more dangerous journeys in his life.

"If those ones did not kill me, this one cannot," he thought.

After a few hours, they arrived at a rock.

"This is the rock on which a prophet in the temple once died," the guide said. "Some say it was from poison. There are also rumors that he placed heavy curses on his town and its people for daring to embarrass him by banishing him from the community. We must stare less at it because our people believe that staring means the curse can begin to affect you immediately." Uncle Sam looked away.

In a few minutes, they reached the temple. They met an old, unkempt priest sleeping.

"He can sleep for several days without waking up," the guide said. Uncle Sam did not understand how anyone could sleep for several days without waking up if such a person was not dead. "This is power," the guide continued. "He has traveled into the world of the spirits. No one can wake him up except with certain rituals."

"How then can he be woken up?" Uncle Sam asked.

"Several years ago," the guide said, "my father, who met him before, told me how to wake him up if ever I found him in this state. Let me get to the root of this rock; I hope to find a big calabash, which contains some herbs. I will just dig my two hands into it, place both hands to the sky and then come and touch him with both hands. He will wake up. But he might get angry and make all of us unconscious."

"Let's do it then," Uncle Sam said.

"What if I don't wake up again?" the guide asked surprised that Sam did not seem to have understood his earlier statement.

"Why won't you wake up?" Uncle Sam asked.

"You will wake up," Pa Ikedi assured Okoro.

Okoro summoned courage and initiated the activities he had explained earlier. He went to the foot of the rock and, shortly after, came back with outstretched arms dripping liquid. He proceeded to touch the old priest with his dripping hands, and immediately Okoro became unconscious.

The old priest woke up and, without uttering a word, brought out a pigeon from one of the calabashes at the temple, strangled it and poured the blood into Okoro's ears, mouth and nostrils. Okoro slowly began regaining consciousness.

"Leave him. He will wake up whenever he wants to. He has to sleep," the priest said. "You have come to know about the curse, right?"

"How did he know why we are here?" Uncle Sam whispered to Pa Ikedi, startled that the old priest could be that accurate and exact.

"Why won't he know? He knows things even before you think about them," Pa Ikedi replied quietly.

"Answer me," the old priest demanded.

"Yeeeees, wise old one," Pa Ikedi replied. "The chick does not recognize the hawk so it thinks about playing with it as a fellow mother hen; only its mother knows it as dangerous. Please pardon the mistake of my young man." Pa Ikedi gestured as he asked for leniency on behalf of Uncle Sam, whose countenance vacillated between anxiety and outright dread at the thought of being declared guilty of any punishable offence.

"I can see that," the priest said nodding continuously. "Do you really want to know about what you asked for?" At this point, Uncle Sam started feeling scared and wanted to start heading back home.

"Yes," Pa Ikedi responded. "That's why we endured the land mines to be here with you, wise old one."

"Your son is afraid," the old one said.

"He has to be wise, old one. The child must get scared if he gets to the point of danger."

"You are right, my brother. But only the brave can kill a lion. I will take you both on a journey where you will find out about the curse.

"First, let me warn that nothing must scare you in this temple. Whatever scares you in this place can consume you as well. Second, anything you see from now on, you must never tell anyone who is not here today. Whatever you see or hear, pretend like you never saw or heard it, okay?" The priest spoke in a matter-of-fact tone, directing his gaze towards Uncle Sam, letting him know that the comments were more for him than Pa Ikedi.

"Yes, sir," Uncle Sam said.

The old priest brought out his flute and blew it so forcefully, his checks puffed up with air and out came a screeching sound that was guttural and unnatural. A huge python crawled slowly into their presence. Uncle Sam's eyes widened. He had never seen a python that big with his bare eyes before. The python regally and ceremoniously circled them three times and started slithering back.

"Now, the gods said I can share the knowledge with you," the old one said.

"Is the python a god?" Uncle Sam asked.

"Which python?" the old one countered.

"The one that just left."

"Do pythons answer the call of a flute?" the old one queried. "If a python ever came here, you would have been eaten up by now. What you saw was the gods. If not for their magnanimity, you would never get here safely. People have died trying to get to this temple because the gods did not like them. Unlike pythons, the gods do not bite."

Uncle Sam found it hard to believe what the old man said. He sat motionless, ruminating over the information he had just heard. "Is it possible that what I saw with my own eyes a few moments ago was truly not a snake but a god?" he thought. He could not find the conviction in him to believe this strange story.

From a black pot, the man brought out a small cloth tied up with something inside it. He gave it to Uncle Sam and said, "Before you sleep tonight, rub it on your face three times. You can go now."

The old man hit Okoro hard and said, "Haven't you woken up?"

Okoro woke up. He could not believe he had slept so long.

"Take them back to where they are coming from," the old man said. "Take this to show you the way and guide you safely."

Okoro collected the object, which looked like several items tied together: a bird feather, red cloth, tumors and other things he could not identify.

"For you," the old man said, pointing to Uncle Sam. "When you are coming back here, just rub the powder I gave you and the gods will allow you pass to this point in safety."

*   *   *

The old king was lying helpless as a result of failing health. His children, wives and numerous concubines sat beside him hoping that he would recover soon.

As they all gathered, his eldest son, Jigbi, exclaimed, "My dear king, you must not leave us like this without a word about what to do. If you leave us like this, we will all be confused and your kingdom will be in disarray."

"At least take one morsel of food to keep you strong," one of the wives said.

On hearing this, the old king gradually mustered the strength and made an effort to rise and sit up. His failing health was telling on his face. The veins that had become obvious on his skull were clear reflections of how many sunsets he had seen in his eventful life, most of which he spent building his kingdom.

"Carefully, old king," one of the children said as the old man held on to his failing strength to sit up. His muscles were not as strong as they used to be. He sat up slowly.

The old king brought out a brass-like object from under his bed and said, "There shall be a pact between our community kings and the priests of the temple at Jiga. So have it.

"This brass-like object will be used to make the king's crown, of which the priest shall be the custodian. Whenever the king passes on at any time, the brass crown must return to the priest before nightfall."

At that moment, the priest, who the old king had earlier sent for, came in. The king looked at the priest and asked, "How did the oracle say we should construct the crown?"

The priest said, "They have said that the bead-like snake lives among the cocoa plantations. It has fallen in love with cocoa, not because it eats cocoa but because the former protects it from the attacks of its enemies and it in turns protects the cocoa from the invading insects and birds."

"The priest may wish to interpret the language of the oracle to the uninitiated," the old king said.

"You are right, my king," the priest said. "What the oracle said is in parables. But I will interpret as simply as I can.

"The oracle simply said, like the bead-like snake and the cocoa, the palace and the temple are two parts of the same entity that need each other at every time. The bead-like snake can sometimes get angry with the cocoa, and the cocoa gets angry with the bead-like snake. If both fight, insects and birds will invade the cocoa plantation and there will be no cover anymore for the bead-like snake.

"So the oracle is saying that, no matter what, the palace must never get angry with the temple, and the temple must never get angry with the palace because, if that ever happens, it shall be tantamount to sacrilege for which the gods of the land must be appeased.

"For this ritual, we will gather herbs the oracle has prescribed. We will burn them to ashes. We will get a large male snail and burn it with its shell and pour the first half into a small black pot and put it into the brass crown for all future kings and Queens to wear as the seal of authority.

"The second half we shall pour into the staff of all future priests, which shall be given to them before their first entry into the temple. This shall be a sign of covenant between the palace and the temple. The remaining shall be placed in the custody of the priest to make totems to be used only on special occasions on behalf of the community. After this is done, we must break the black pot into fragments."

The old king slowly lay back on the bed and said, "The totems." The children really did not understand what he meant. After saying that, he shut his eyes and finally slept. Because they saw it coming, no one cried.

* * *

It was several years later, and the bell was ringing. Nobody had ever heard the town crier sound his bell in the dead of the night, and he rarely made his announcements by night. Calling people's names loudly at night was considered a taboo because malevolent spirits could cash in on the action to harm the person being called.

"First," the town crier said, "I am extremely sorry for calling you out at this time of night. This is very unusual. But what must be said at night should never wait till morning."

"What is it?" the villagers asked impatiently as every one of them felt annoyed at being disturbed.

"The great elephant of our clan, the conquering lion of all the seven mountains and villages of our clan, the great python that walks through the forests oblivious of the dangers therein, the king over spirits and men, the king of our community has joined his ancestors tonight."

"No!" the villagers exclaimed.

"The palace has asked me to warn you that for the next seven days, no one, indigenes or strangers, must be seen outside when the moon is out. This is because the king must be committed to the earth in seven days. If your goat goes missing during these seven days, please look for it. If your sheep goes missing, please look for them. But if your child goes missing, it is futile to look for them. Have I spoken well?"

"Yes, you have."

The villagers began picking up their children and shutting their doors early from that day until the duration of the days of ritual observance leading up to the king's burial ceremony and final interment.

After a few days, one of the chiefs visited the palace. He was looking for an old woman who had witnessed the activities of many years, during which time three or four kings had come and gone. The woman knew many secrets surrounding the palace and the community. The chief found the old lady taking a nap.

"Greetings, old one," the chief said. "It looks as if you are tired."

"Tired? If I was tired, I would be in my house. I'm only relaxing," the old woman said.

"I hope you haven't forgotten about our last discussion," the chief said.

"We have discussed so many things in the past months, which one?" the old woman asked, trying to recall it.

"About the vacant kingship."

"Oh, that?"

"Yes."

"I have already told you that our king cannot amass wealth," the old woman said. "There are certain mysteries that will prevent any king in our land from amassing wealth."

"Why is that? Are they cursed?"

"Even if you are a palace chief," the old woman told him, "there are certain mysteries you can never find out. My closeness to the elder made me know some things, but there are too many mysteries around it that you will never understand. If you want to amass wealth, stay away from the palace of our community."

"You still haven't told me why. Because the king-elect is my friend and I supported him to the throne, I want him to amass a lot of wealth."

"In that case, tell him not to take any oath before the priest at the temple. It's dangerous. Don't say I did not warn you. You won't understand, but I warned you," the old woman said on a note of finality.

The king-elect in his traditional seclusion sat with royal clothes on. Legend had it that the clothes symbolized purity of intent and the humility expected of the king at all times once he had been invested to the throne of his fathers.

The king-elect was on his seat when the chief rushed in.

"Greetings, my king," the chief said, bowing.

"You are old enough to be my father, chief. Why do you bow before me?" the king-elect asked in surprise, not being used to such courtesies from more elderly people.

"That's the way it's done. Once you become king, you are king over the young and old, rich and poor, witches and wizards, and everyone.

"Now, about what we discussed the last time, my king –"

"You mean about how I can amass wealth while on the throne?"

"Yes. You must never take any oath in the temple administered by the priest."

"Okay," the king-elect replied. He knew the chief had been a major supporter in his quest to be named king-elect.

On the seventh day, the new king was to be invested through the oath-taking ritual. All was set and the community was agog, everyone feverishly anticipating the great festivities that were to follow.

The priest said to the king-elect, "Now, we are getting to the crux of your initiation, which will make you wear the crown of your fathers. I've anxiously waited for this period so that your reign and authority could begin and so that I could truly find some rest from the activities of these last few days. But first things first ...

"I will make an incision on your back and you will take the sacred oath of allegiance to the throne of our ancestors and obedience to the time-honored principle of humanity and modesty –"

But the king-elect interjected, "What do you mean I should take an oath? I am not taking any oath. I am not accepting any incision on my body. All these practices are ancient and outdated and I, Gobi, the new king of a great community, have decided to abolish such unprogressive practices. This initiation is over."

"We are not done yet," the priest said.

The king-elect brought out a sharp knife and pointed it at the priest's face. "What did I say?"

"You said, 'We have finished the initiation,'" the priest said remaining unruffled.

The king-elect returned the dagger into the white cloth he had tied to his waist as part of his regalia and walked out on the priest. Still unruffled, the priest watched the king-elect go; then he glanced at his disciples and said, "Is this our king?"

Gobi was sworn in as the new king the next day in an elaborate ceremony that had people from all walks of life in attendance. The only obvious absence was the priest or anyone from the temple to represent him. One of the chiefs who had sponsored his ascendance performed the ceremonial duty of final coronation in their stead. Since it was the traditional duty of the temple priest to carry out the coronation, an excuse had to be offered to explain his absence. The official explanation given by the palace was that the priest was "indisposed" and could not therefore be present to perform the sacred function. Most people did not ask questions about the priest's absence since they were carried away by the merriment. The chief, in a hurry, went back to the old woman in the palace immediately after the coronation of the new king. He met the old lady taking a nap as usual in the lobby of the palace.

"If this woman is too tired," he said, "she should go home and retire rather than suffer herself here."

The old woman woke up and laughed.

"Old one, you weren't sleeping?"

"Non-salaried posts like mine do not need retirement. I just pray that the great gods of our land will give us all peaceful transitions to the world beyond."

"Please forgive me, old one." The chief took his seat and said, "Something has been bothering me since our last discussion and that's why I ran to you again. I thought you were asleep."

"I wasn't sleeping. That's how I get a lot of revelations about several mysteries. If the toad is running in the afternoon, it's either pursuing something or something is pursuing it," the old woman said. "So, what are you after or what is after you?"

"Please, forgive me once again," the chief said.

"I have forgiven you. I have heard and seen so many insults in my lifetime. I have become used to all that at my age." She added, "Our lives are very complex; no one can fathom the depth and the fullness." Then the old woman stared into the chief's eyes. "I hope there is no problem this time?"

The chief drew close to the old woman as if trying to whisper in her ear, and then in a conspiratorial tone, he said, "It's about our last discussion on the king's oath-taking. You didn't tell me the consequences of not taking the oath."

"You did not ask me either. I only answered the questions I was asked," the old lady said.

"Now, can you then tell me the consequences because this new king did not take the oath at the temple."

"Ah!" the old woman shouted unguardedly before covering her mouth. She looked over her shoulders to be sure no one was eavesdropping around the palace.

"Do you know that's a sacrilege? Do you know the implications of that?" the old woman asked.

"We have done this, so what are the consequences?" the chief demanded.

"There are several dangers for any king who does not take the oath at the temple. The first, the priest must never use the totems during the reign of the king and during any disagreement between the palace and the temple. If that should happen, the king must go to the market square, dance naked and die. Such a king would never be given a royal burial and his lineage will never be king in our community for life.

"The second danger is that calamity upon calamity will befall the community during the king's reign. Sacrilege will be committed involving human lives. Values will be transported away from the community to distant lands, and calamities will befall those places too. Things such as strange diseases and natural disasters will become regular occurrences within the community. The sun will start to emerge from the earth, rivers will overflow their bounds, fire will emerge from water to consume whole villages and things like that. The calamities may take generations to cure," the old man said.

"Old one. You are heartless! So, you kept all these secrets from us all the while? You are a very wicked, old-for-nothing hag!"

The old woman was beginning her response to the chief but the chief walked out in annoyance. The old lady looked on in dismay.

*　*　*

Uncle Sam woke up drenched in sweat. "It was a dream! What sort of strange dream is this?"

Then he remembered and lifted one of his pillows; he found the concoction the old man from the temple at Jiga had given him during their last visit.

"I have to go back to the old one," he said. "This dream is strange."

 **APPEASING THE GODS**

Pa Ikedi needed to take his drugs as recommended by the physician, so he would not be joining Uncle Sam on the journey to the temple at Jiga. Uncle Sam again opted for public transport to Momuregbo village because he had properly understood the directions to the village.

When Okoro took Uncle Sam to the temple, this time, the priest was not asleep.

"Come in my children," a voice said as they got to the entrance of the vast temple.

They walked in.

"You've seen something my son," the old priest said.

"Yes, I did. But I –" Uncle Sam started to offer some reservations.

"– you didn't understand what it was. Am I right?" the old priest asked, interrupting him.

"Yes, wise one," Uncle Sam said. Once again he wondered how the old priest knew what he had not yet uttered. He felt it necessary to talk less and listen more.

"What you saw is one of the well-kept secrets of the gods. They've not shown that to anyone outside this temple," the priest said. "They have told you of the sacrilege committed against them. They have told you about the consequences of the sacrilege against them. These will live with you mortals for a while until you are ready to perform the sacrifices."

"What will the sacrifices cost?" Uncle Sam asked.

"The sacrifices will cost the heads, livers and hearts of seven kings," the old priest said.

"That's too much, old one."

"So was shedding the blood of the innocent on this land, so was taking our lads forcefully in enslavement, so was grabbing the king's throne without authorization from the temple!

"The sacrifices will be great, my son. But whether you like it or not, you will come here for it. Today, we are talking about seven kings; next time it may get even more severe. Our gods do not forget!"

"I shall go now," Uncle Sam said.

As Uncle Sam departed the temple precinct with Okoro, his mind was filled with thoughts of his fearsome dream.

"Indeed the sacrilege must have been immense," he thought. Clearly, the gods of the land were averse to the ways and manners of the leadership in the various communities in the land; they had elevated corruption, nepotism, materialism, mediocrity and other vices. How indeed could there be progress in the land. The leadership had come to assume the status of gods. They had taken over the rights and privileges reserved only for the gods and the ancestors.

"How could there be progress in the land?" he asked himself again and again.

"But what can I do?" he queried. "Why me?" Finding no answers, Uncle Sam walked on in quiet contemplation, Okoro trudging on ahead of him.

His heart was heavy and he experienced more agitation rising within him. How come? How far? Who's next? Where else? All questions, but no answers. What next?

And that was when a thought came forcefully to him. This second visit within a month was motivated by the revelations he had through the influence of the sacred concoction in the small bottle the priest of the temple at Jiga had given him.

"Since every effect has a cause," he thought, "all problems have different solutions."

"There must certainly be a way out of these problems. The gods who revealed the problems of past ages to me will surely let me into the secrets that will bring us solutions," he reasoned.

As the revelation dawned on him, he quickened his steps. He could not wait to get home, being fully assured now that revelations of the way forward out of this quagmire would come the same way. If he got home safely, he would sleep. Then he would know. Yes, the gods of the land would let him into the processes of regenerating the land.

Now, my ancestors will take you through the next chapter of this book. Please let them. Keep an open mind. Remove all doubts and prepare to be marveled.

Our ancestral spirit will guide you, astrally project you, through the unspeakable sacrilege committed in time past that is so grave it cannot be written or spoken of until an appeasement is completed.

Now, close this book and put it under your pillow and repeat the words "Amadi Oha" three times after which you are not to offer any more words to anyone before you sleep.

Keep your thoughts away from wantons, proceed to sleep and chapter 11 will be revealed to you tonight in your *Ofeorie* dream ...

CPSIA information can be obtained
at www.ICGtesting.com
Printed in the USA
BVHW071441220419
546167BV00002B/432/P